CHAPTER: 4

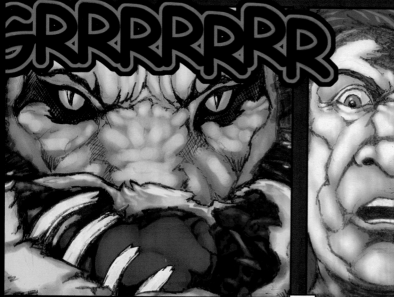

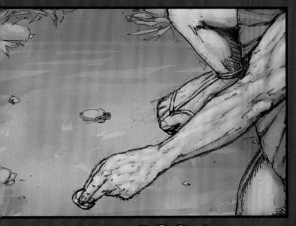

SWOOOSHH

THW-ACK

WHOA...

AHH

THUNK

CRACK

WHO'S THERE?

DAVID.

YOU CAN KEEP IT.

BY NEXT WEEK WE'LL BE IN HEBRON TRAINING WITH SWORD AND SPEAR. THAT'S THE WAY TO KILL A PHILISTINE.

THANKS, OZEM.

Later that day David practiced with the sling...

THAP

THOMP

BAA-A-A

THOMP

...but it was not easy to use.

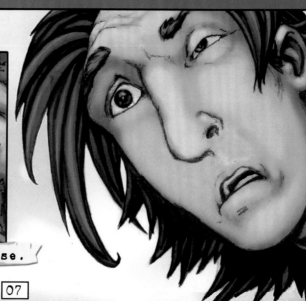

SEVENTY FIVE, SEVENTY SIX, SEVENTY SEVEN...

HUH? ONLY SEVENTY EIGHT.

DAD'S GOING TO BE SO UPSET IF I DON'T FIND THAT MISSING SHEEP.

WHAT'S THIS?

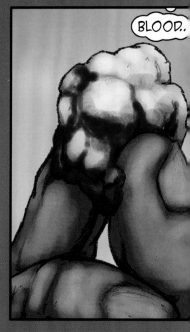

BLOOD..

THE BLOOD LEADS INTO THE WOODS.

YES FATHER, BUT...

SO, YOU WERE NOT WATCHING THE SHEEP AND NOW ONE IS MISSING. AND A BEAST MUST HAVE TAKEN IT. IS THAT IT?

YOU DISAPPOINT ME, DAVID. YOUR BROTHERS ARE BUSY WITH OTHER THINGS AND SO AM I. THE RESPONSIBILITY OF TENDING TO THE FLOCK IS YOURS. OUR FAMILY DEPENDS UPON THAT.

I'M SORRY, FATHER.

THE SLING.

I WILL NOT HAVE YOU PLAYING WITH THIS WHEN YOU HAVE FAMILY DUTIES.

DO YOU UNDERSTAND?

YES, FATHER.

GOOD. NOW NO MORE GAMES AND CHILDISH FANTASIES. TAKE THE BREAD FROM YOUR MOTHER THEN RETURN TO THE SHEEP.

THIS IS FRESH.

THANKS. IT SMELLS GOOD.

BE CAREFUL OUT THERE, DAVID.

YES, MOTHER.

DO YOU THINK HE COULD HAVE SPOKEN TRUE?

THERE ARE NO BEASTS HERE. ONLY BOYS MAKING EXCUSES.

...but the lion grew furious, for it was not accustomed to giving up a meal once it had been caught.

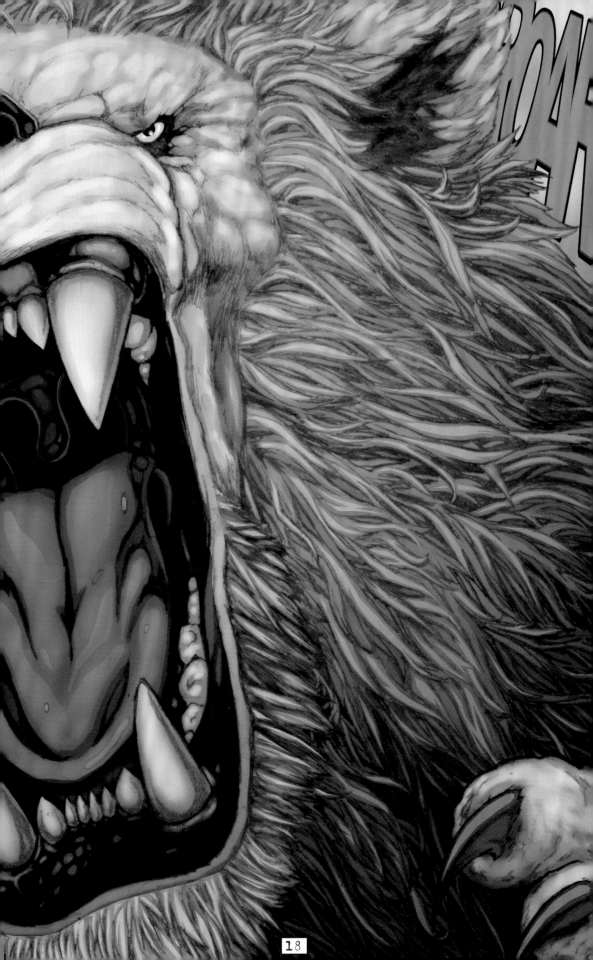

ROARR

SISHSCRATCH

David's wounds were severe...

...and his body was exhausted...

ARAGH!

ROARR

GRRAR

...but he saw his chance.

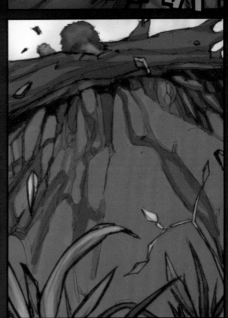

RRRARR

Now it was the lion who lay wounded.

R-YOWLL

GALLRP

RAAHH!

YOU HAVE CLAWS AND MIGHTY TEETH, BUT WHAT GOOD HAVE THEY DONE YOU?

YOU HAVE TRIED TO DESTROY ME, BUT NOW YOU ARE DESTROYED!

KRAK

THE END

(THE RISE OF DAVID
Pt.4)

SS

HAND ME THAT WRENCH, SON.

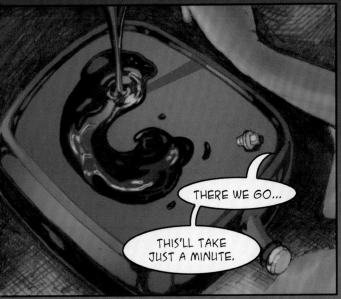

THERE WE GO...

THIS'LL TAKE JUST A MINUTE.

Dad always changes his own oil...

I think that's cool...

He's the only dad I know who still does it himself...

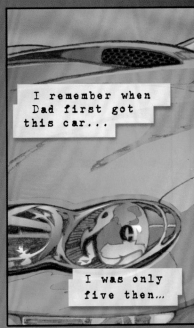

I remember when Dad first got this car...

I was only five then...

I thought it was awesome...

Still do...

Only 375 in the world like this, but...

He had it special ordered from the factory...

...this one's special he'd say...

Dad'd take us out "cruisin" on Sunday afternoons. My brother, Bill, complained the back seats were too cramped...

But I liked the way it felt...

HAND ME THAT RAG, WOULD YOU, SON.

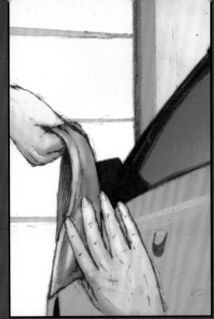

He always kept it so clean...

PASS ME THE OIL, ANDY.

HERE YA GO.

THANKS.

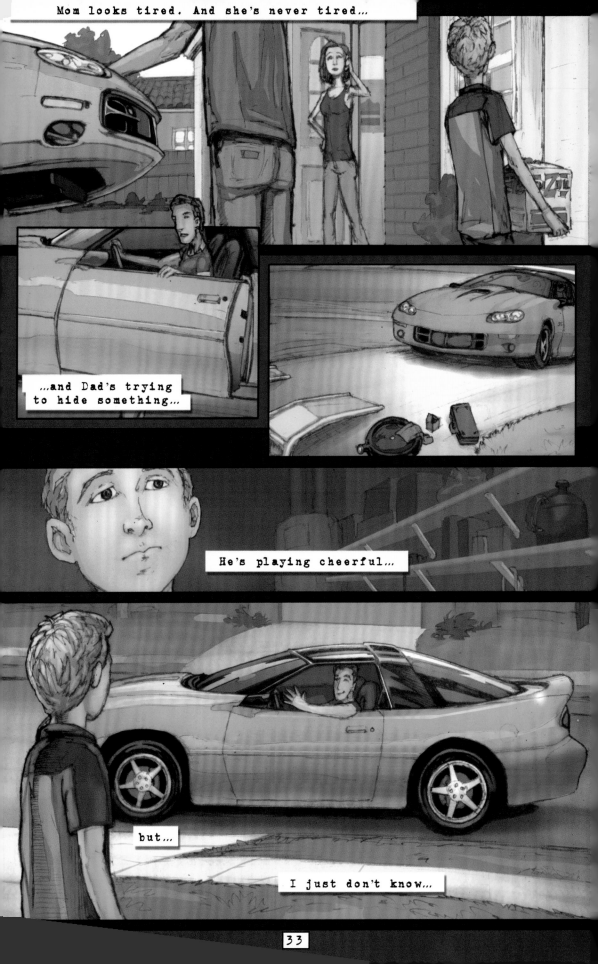

WHERE'S KEVIN BEEN?

HE'S GROUNDED.

BUT HE'S FREE AGAIN TOMORROW.

WHAT DID HE DO?

HE GOT IN A FIGHT AT SCHOOL.

AH-HUH. I HOPE EVERYONE'S OKAY.

THEY'RE FINE.

WHO'S THE OTHER BOY?

JASON.

JASON CALLED KEVIN A BOOGER PICKER AND KEVIN CALLED JASON A MOMMA'S BOY!

IS JASON A MOMMA'S BOY?

YEAH, BUT HE DOESN'T WANT EVERYONE TO KNOW!

HEY, I'M READY.

ANDY, GUESS WHICH RESTAURANT IS GONNA HAVE THE *JUSTICE AVENGER* PROMOTION?

DUH, IT'S THE *BURGER BANDIT.* THAT'S BEEN ALL OVER THEIR WEBSITE FOR A WEEK.

THERE'LL BE FIVE ACTION FIGURES, A JET-CYCLE, AND GAME CARDS.

YEP, AND I BET YOU'LL WANT THE WHOLE SET, HUH?

WELL, YOU BETTER GET YOUR *HAPPY DEALS* WHEN I AIN'T AROUND...

'CAUSE THE ONLY TOY YOU'RE GETTING FROM ME IS THE STUPID *ROBOT.*

GOOD 'CAUSE I WAS HOPING FOR A WHOLE ARMY OF *KILLER ROBOTS!*

Back at home.

HEY BILL, CAN YOU HELP ME FOR A SEC?

CAN'T I CHANGE FIRST?

IT'LL JUST TAKE A MINUTE.

HEY BILL...

MOM, I'M GOING OUT, OKAY?

BE BACK BY DARK...

FORGET THEM...

ANDY! WAIT UP!

HEY, THERE'S YOUR BRO.

WANNA WATCH 'EM PLAY?

NO. I'D JUST WIND UP FETCHING BALLS.

DUDE! WHAT'S YOUR PROB? SCRAPE A KNEE NOW YOU WANNA GO HOME?

SORRY. I'M IN A LOUSY MOOD. SOME'INS UP WITH MOM & DAD, BUT THEY WON'T TELL.

NO. THAT'S NOT TRUE.

THEY JUST WON'T TELL *ME*.

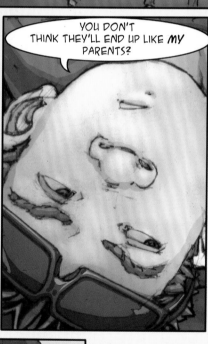

YOU DON'T THINK THEY'LL END UP LIKE *MY* PARENTS?

NO, MAN! DON'T EVEN SAY THAT.

IT'S NOTHING LIKE THAT.

'CAUSE, HEY. IF THEY DO, YOU'LL MAKE OUT LIKE A BANDIT ON CHRISTMAS AND BIRTHDAYS.

JUST PLAYIN', DUDE. YOU GOT THE COOLEST PARENTS I KNOW. YOUR MA'S ALWAYS MAKIN' *COOKIES!*

YEAH, AND DAD'S ALWAYS TAKIN' US TO THE...

THWAK

46

BILL, DAD'S GONNA GO OUT OF BUSINESS...

...AND YOU KNEW...

YOU KNEW AND DIDN'T TELL ME.

I KNOW DAD TOLD YOU. I SAW HIM. I'M NOT STUPID.

I KNOW YOU'RE NOT STUPID, ANDY.

BUT DAD'S NOT GOING OUT OF BUSINESS.

HE'LL BE FINE.

WE'RE ALL GOING TO BE OKAY.

The End: Chapter 5

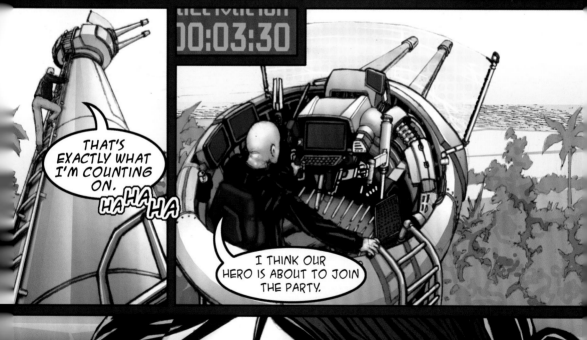

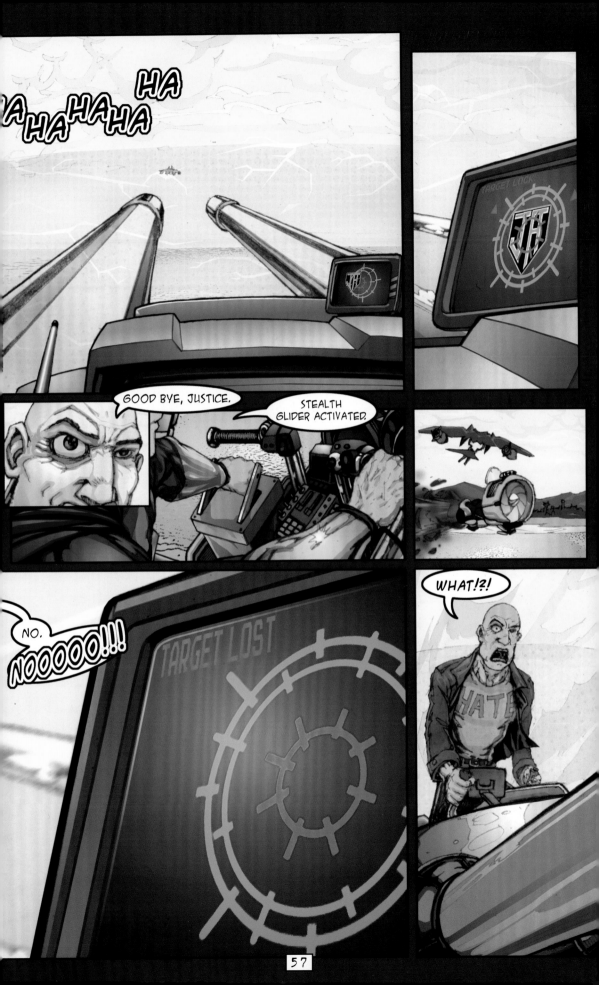

YOU'RE IN RANGE! FIRE!!!

WREEEKSH

e Field Deactivation
TIMER_00:01:30

OORRRRRR

INCOMING!
INCOMING!
INCOMING!

RRARHH

HA HA HA HA

THEY DIDN'T EXPLODE! POOR JUSTICE AVENGER'S SHOOTING BLANKS!!!

CRASH

WHAAA???

RROAR

NO!

.d Deactivation
ER_00:00:59

I HATE LIZARDS!

Ce Field Deactivation
TIMER_00:00:20

KA-TAT TAT TAT

ARREE

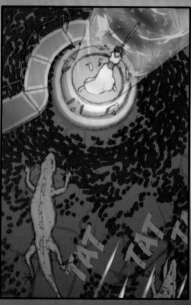

HAHAHA HAHA

Deactivation
_00:00:05

AHRRRRR AHRRRR

GRRUN

Field Deactivated
MER_00:00:00

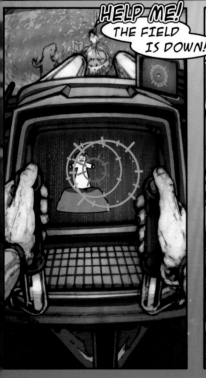

HELP ME! THE FIELD IS DOWN!

RUIIIURRRR

TA

THIS IS NOT THE ONE I SEEK.

STEP ASIDE, ELIAB.

ABINADAB, COME FORTH.

NOR HAVE I CHOSEN THIS ONE.

YOUR THIRD.

SHAMAH, STAND TRUE.

THIS IS NOT HE.

THE NEXT.

HIM! THAT MAN! WHERE HAVE YOU HIDDEN HIM?

WHAT ARE YOU LOOKING AT?

HUSBAND PLEASE!

AHH!

SLOOSH

DOES HE STILL COWER LIKE A DOG IN THE BATH?

SLISHH

THIS IS TREACHERY! I SHOULD KILL YOU BOTH!

NO, FATHER! YOU KNOW NOT WHAT YOU SAY.

DO NOT TELL ME MY MIND, BOY. DO YOU THINK I HAVE NOT HEARD THE WHISPERING?

YOUR PRESENCE HERE IS A DISGRACE. SUCH INSOLENCE IN MY OWN HOUSE.

HEA-HEA-HEA-H

AAEHHRRKRR

DAVID, SON OF JESSE, COME. KNEEL BEFORE ME.

THE LORD OF OUR SALVATION HAS CALLED YOU FOR A SPECIAL PURPOSE.

YOU SHALL BE *HIS* CHAMPION. THE WILL OF THE ONE TRUE *GOD* WILL DWELL, EVER, IN YOUR SOUL.

I ANOINT YOU FOR *GOD*, BY *HIS* COMMAND.

...and the Spirit of God came upon David in power and might.

NOW ARISE LORD DAVID.

BUT I AM NOT A GREAT MAN THAT YOU SHOULD CALL ME LORD.

THAT IS WHERE YOU ARE MISTAKEN.

That evening David played and sung.

...AND THE BOY WITH THE HARP, NEVER HAVE I HEARD SUCH A VOICE. AND HE PLAYS WITH GREAT SKILL. WHO IS HIS FATHER?

THE SAME ONE WE HAVE ALREADY SPOKEN OF.

HE IS THE SON OF JESSE. AND FEEL NO SHAME AT YOUR HYPNOTISM, FOR ALL SOULS ARE LIFTED WHEN THE YOUNG ONE PLAYS...

...AND MIGHTY IS HE.

YES?

TO BE SURE, FOR NOT LONG AGO THE BOY SLAIN A LION IN THE FIELDS WITH NOTHING BUT A CLUB OF WOOD.

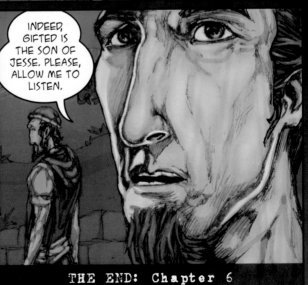

INDEED, GIFTED IS THE SON OF JESSE. PLEASE, ALLOW ME TO LISTEN.

THE END: Chapter 6

WWW.OLDTIMESTORIES.COM

ANDY™

$7.50

Title: ANDY Book 1, Retail Edition
Publisher: Old Time Stories
Author/Artist: Joseph Mazerac
Content appropriateness: Ages 9 and up
ISBN: 978-0-9792770-0-9
Retail Price: $9.99

Special Edition
Signed by Joseph Mazerac

$10.00

Young people discover a gateway to the Bible through what they like most... comic books. Combine the book and Teacher's Guide for the classroom to excite and inspire children to discover the relevance and wonder of the Bible.

In ANDY Book 1, readers will enjoy short Justice Avenger adventures as Andy and his friends play and have fun. But it's not all playtime. Andy must also face the real world, with school, chores, and a big brother. One day as Andy's dad studies the Bible, Andy starts asking questions. His father begins telling Andy stories of the first Kings of Israel. Andy's imagination kicks into high gear and the readers see biblical stories through his amazing imagination. Full of wonderful color illustrations, ANDY is sure to engage any young reader.

Highlighted in CBA Retailer & Resources

$15.00

JUSTICE AVENGER

$18.00

ANDY, Book 1 Teacher's GUIDE: Six carefully planned, interactive lessons that are sure to engage even the most energetic students. The guide was designed to present biblical stories and concepts in a way that grasps students' interest and helps them to remember what they've learned. The lessons explore the comic's exciting characters, while continuously helping students to relate the biblical content to their own lives.

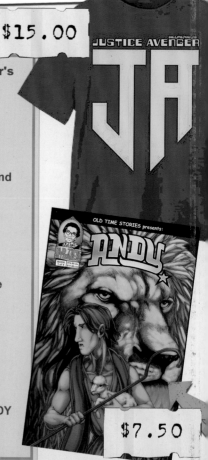

$7.50

Teacher's Guide includes:
- Six carefully planned and detailed lessons to be used in conjunction with ANDY, Book 1
- A CD containing easily printable worksheets and the 96 page ANDY graphic novel all in high quality digital format
- Bonus materials including fun Biblical facts, games, and maps